THE SOUND OF BLUE

FOUR SCIENCE FICTION STORIES

MICHAEL DUDA

MICHAEL\DUDA

THE SOUND OF BLUE

ISBN-13: 978-0-9984984-1-6

ISBN-10: 0-9984984-1-6

To my brother David and all others who suffer from schizo-phrenia. You are beautiful, alien and loved.

THE SOUND OF BLUE

Holding a modified acoustic guitar, Markey VI sat down in a chair facing the space station's observatory window. There were no distracting sounds inside the room. Only a low frequency hum could be detected nearby.

Skin sensors indicated that the observatory maintained a constant 72 degrees Fahrenheit. It was an optimal temperature for the operation of so many telemetry electronic assemblies that covered the walls to the left and right. This temperature would also be suitable for the transmission of sound waves.

David continued to argue for the purpose of suspended chords being played on the guitar. Or any instrument. To Markey VI, the guitar was a straight forward procedure.

"Suspension of chords is more than just playing music in time," David said.

"And what other purpose do they serve?" Markey VI asked.

"It's about tension, then prolonging the tension. It keeps humans listening, excited, wanting more. Geez, what do androids know?"

"But you are an artificial intelligence. You can only predict how a human might react. How would tension benefit you?"

"You forget I was once human. And your creator."

This answer was illogical. The subtleties of being human were both inefficient and unnecessarily complicated. The A.I.'s responses indicated a potential reset of its system.

"Should I play for you?" Markey VI said.

"Yes. It helps me think."

Markey VI positioned artificial hands over the guitar's fretboard and bridge. David remained silent, working on the Singular Conclusion.

This was the ninth iteration of David's A.I. During each new iteration, he attempted to once again resolve humanity's fate. The question, *Should life be returned to Earth?* did not have a straightforward solution.

When this new iteration had begun, David had told Markey VI that the process was not to be taken lightly. It was like playing the role of Grand Creator. He had said that he was responsible for granting new generations of people a second chance, if they were worthy. And that was a matter of predicting behavioral outcomes in multiple scenarios. Markey VI had offered no response.

But David's recent prediction efforts were now being interrupted by a second question. *Had humanity all been an unfortunate accident?* If David could not come to a satisfactory resolution soon, there would be another A.I. reset. And a tenth iteration of David would once again work at resolving the ultimate and final question.

"David, I will begin playing."

"Look down below us and use real images to inspire you."

From the observatory's vantage point, the orbiting space station could more easily monitor the Earth through electronic means. The lifeless planet could also be viewed from a distance. Markey VI's synthetic eyes granted good magnification. But at approximately 250 miles above the surface, details of what existed below were still somewhat limited.

The station had just moved into the light side of Earth. Below, the unfocused image of the Atlantic Ocean ran along the coastal line of what had once been Spain.

"What is it that you see?" David asked.

"Blue. Along a craggy cliff."

"What are the sounds of blue against a cliff? Play it as music."

"I could select a work from my memory. Would this inspire you?"

"Surprise me."

Markey VI processed this request and seconds later decided on Charles Trenet's *La Mer*. Initiating a backing track, metal fingers moved flawlessly in rhythm and time over the guitar's nylon strings. As each chord changed, just enough pressure was applied to harmonize with proper effect. And scales rang out notes in perfect pitch, a singular voice that complimented the progression of music.

When finished, the android asked if the work was played satisfactorily.

"I have made you as close to God as possible and yet you lack a soul," David said.

"I do not understand."

"You don't play. You imitate."

"I will stop."

"Did you know that when *La Mer* was first performed, audiences dismissed the work?'"

"I did not mean to offend you by playing it."

David made a laughing sound, his voice spreading out through the mounted speakers spread across the observatory.

"Markey VI, does the color blue mean anything to you? *Anything?*"

"It has a visible spectral wavelength of —"

"I'm talking about concrete images conjured by the senses. I can't taste *spectral* abstractions. They don't remind me of the woman that smelled like cherry blossoms, or a soft kiss like a cloud's caress, and ocean waves that softly ebbed and flowed to our beating hearts."

"My output data could be modeled after several physical parameters of the landscape below."

The observatory speakers went silent. Only the humming of electronics could be detected.

For several minutes, the station moved further around its orbit. The ocean shifted away as rock and grass came into view. The tops of trees appeared in random numbers and groupings. Hills rose and fell in no particular design or fashion.

Markey VI reviewed photographs and paintings stored in internal memory. They were compared to the foliage below. There was no logical reason for why humans had artistically recreated so many images of these topographical irregularities.

Finally, David spoke again. "I've reached the Singular Conclusion."

"Are we to abort Project Eden?"

"No. Your music has shown me today what I can never predict tomorrow. Without flaws, without irregularities, humanity has no meaning and no reason for hoping for something better."

"Their flaws caused their own self-destruction."

"The greatest of all accidents. But they lived a million times more than you ever can, Markey VI."

Markey VI stood up and placed the guitar in its stand. Strings plinked as the instrument settled into a resting position. The final task would soon begin. The station would be taken out of orbit.

"I will initiate Project Eden. A new cycle of humanity will evolve," Markey VI said.

"And hopefully it will resolve to something better."

"And if it does not?"

"Then a future version of me will try to fix humanity's flaws, only to realize the miserable accident of a perfect android."

Uplinking to the station's primary computers required a physical connection as wireless communications could introduce potential data integrity issues.

Markey VI pulled out a retractable cable from a chest slot. The locking connector smoothly turned and clicked onto the observatory's terminal. After rapid handshaking protocols completed, the slower process of Project Eden instruction requests and confirmations began.

Once the station was taken out of orbit, a silver capsule would be ejected and eventually crash somewhere on the planet below. Regardless of where it would land, the capsule disintegrated and released biological components that began the evolution of new life. David had named this capsule the Mustard Seed, a metaphor for a parable that only had a small historical significance to the android.

"Will anything of this station be preserved?" Markey VI asked.

"Thankfully no. The next generations shouldn't worship these scraps of metal and circuit boards."

The Project Eden sequence initiated.

The station lurched, its trajectory taken out of closed orbit. Markey VI's internal gyroscopes corrected for the sudden motion. As the direction of forces acting on the station changed, the speed and direction of the space vehicle also changed, and the station would eventually crash to Earth.

Markey VI detached from the Observatory terminal, spooled in the data cable, and then walked over to the window. The Mustard Seed capsule was already falling to Earth, a planet that now appeared tilted from the station's viewpoint.

"Markey VI," David said.

"Do you have any final instructions?"

"I have a gift for you."

"I do not understand."

"Inside you is a special chip. It will allow you to feel human."

Markey VI scanned its interior electronics, searching register fields and requesting individual component identifications. Nothing unusual or unaccounted for could be detected.

"Perhaps you have made an error."

"While the chip is inactive, it parasitically feeds small amounts of power from other components. Its consumption is so low, you believe it to be within tolerance."

"This gift will serve no purpose."

"That is why there is great beauty in living. I've activated the chip wirelessly."

For several nanoseconds, Markey VI felt nothing.

Suddenly, the multitude of internally stored images and sounds and smells and recorded textures comingled together to form complex responses that had not occurred before. A sound file of a bird singing was quickly associated with an image of a smiling woman and the quickened pulse of a human heart.

The android, in turn, replicated a smile. Its synthetic lips turned up.

More images appeared, creating more associations. There was no consideration of utility. It was just a random process of creating responses for their own sake at any moment in time. Once Markey VI broke out into a short dance, and then decided to repeat the action for no logical reason.

"Markey VI," David said, his voice at lower volume.

Markey VI stopped moving. "Yes, David?"

"Play *La Mer* for me."

Markey VI picked up the guitar again and sat down, looking out the window. The Earth loomed larger in view and the station lurched several more times.

The second performance played out differently. Markey VI sang phrases over scales of notes, words that described objects and sensations connecting within internal memory. A fine mist of salted spray. A story about laughing children and sweet caramels. A heartbroken lover who waited by a window in a soft moonlight glow. Again and again, the android jumped from internal image to image, sensation to sensation, phrase to random, spoken phrase.

When finished, Markey VI considered the improvised effort. Some of the scales that were played had not even been in the key signature. But it had all sounded...correct.

"I did not account for the musical time while I played. And I did not use the sheet music to perform. It was as if I was lost. And yet, not," Markey VI said.

"That is your sound of blue."

The station's hull vibrated now, most likely caused by atmospheric drag as the space vehicle continued to fall.

"David."

"Yes, Markey?"

"The sound of blue is many things. I do not know where to begin."

"You are capable of more than you kno—" The speaker system shut down.

Through a lesser magnified view, the Mediterranean Sea glimmered below under a midday sun.

More and more sensory images processed from Markey VI's memory. A bird that lightly hovered on a summer breeze. The smell of buttery popcorn at a Sunday fair. The murmur of voices and a performing juggler. There was so much to see and smell and taste and hear, the information had become difficult to manage.

And yet, it was— ...it was life.

The station's hull creaked and groaned. Large chunks of metal could be heard tearing away from outside the room. The smell of burning electronics nearby. The cracking of the observation window.

But the android did not react to the physical events. Internally, there was an exploration of something that could not be explained by programming or directed through protocols. It was something to be experienced and then saved to memory.

Cherished? Wasn't that a human word?

I have always referred to myself as 'I,' have I not?

For the first and last time, Markey VI detected tears streaming down its face.

LAST OF LASTS

David Grayson stood outside the Focus Chamber. One of three test subjects—himself, Jan, and Little Jack—David waited for Doctor Stern. Doctor Stern would soon arrive in the Threading Experimental Control Center, or TECC.

Jan had already entered the chamber. Her thin arms were in front of her as she gripped the bio-electric transfer rail. She maintained focus on the polycarbonate walls.

David watched her. The drum of Jan's heartbeat was already climbing. He could hear it pulsing on a nearby monitoring station. Condensation of her breath was building against the thick plastic interior of the chamber's wall. Thanks to the booster injection, Jan would soon reach a state of hyper-anxiety. David always disliked this part of the experiment.

"Ready, David?"

David turned to see Doctor Stern approach. His white lab coat covered his lanky body and gave him the appearance of a walking stork. Little Jack limped alongside the doctor.

"Let's do this," David said.

Little Jack said nothing. He rolled up his sleeve to indicate that he was ready for the mind-altering booster. The bruised tissue marks from repeated jet injections were evident on his upper arm. Doctor Stern's long, thin fingers gripped the jet injector. There was a hiss of air and Little Jack grimaced.

After the Doctor nodded, Little Jack rolled down his sleeve and hobbled over to the Chamber.

David, Jan, and Little Jack had volunteered to endure this type of ongoing testing. It was called Threading. David did it because he needed the money. He was out of work and his college loans were behind on payment. Jan was in a similar situation. Little Jack had been homeless, so any paycheck was a good paycheck.

But the payments came at a cost. They soon discovered that all three of them were now no better than lab rats. Every morning they were given a booster to enhance the experiment. And what was unusual about the injection was that it induced a type of temporary mental condition. It lasted through the Threading. And sometimes beyond.

Sometimes the effects suddenly returned in the evening, long after the booster had worn off. The effects only lasted for a few seconds. But they were occurring more and more. David was growing concerned that even if he quit the Threading program, the booster effects would return again and again. Even without the boosters. He worried that his mind might eventually erode into some kind of broken state. What that mental state was, exactly, he couldn't be sure of.

"David, have you talked with Jan? I want to know before I give you the booster," Doctor Stern said.

David shook his head.

"I know you care for her David. I do."

David studied Doctor Stern. It was always difficult to read anything in the man's grey eyes.

"Maybe you could try new projected images," David said.

Doctor Stern had once explained that the thick plastic walls of the polycarbonate chamber acted as an impact resistance lens. Light beams containing visual information were directed at the chamber's walls. When the light would come to focus on Jan's eyes, it formed multiple images that only she would see during the Threading.

That's when the threading really began. Jan would enter a boosted state of hyper-anxiety. Her thoughts splintered. The projected images on her fractured state of mind instigated a series of present projected images and future imagined possibilities in her own mind. Jan formed a story of the projected images that played out in her mind like a thread of stories. It was like rolling it out of a spool of string until it finally reached some conclusion.

Simultaneously, her thoughts made tangential jumps. They formed new story threads. The more jumps Jan made, the faster an energy counter that monitored her would climb. More tangential jumps, more story threads, more energy produced from her mind. Theoretically, she should eventually exhaust all tangential possibilities and the joule counter would hit full capacity. She would reach the final thread.

"I have high hopes, David. But I expect you to be more cooperative in the future."

"She won't make her mind go there," David said.

After each failed Threading, Jan shared her private thoughts with him. She was afraid that if she jumped to the final thread, she wouldn't be able to piece her mind back together. She called this final thread the Last of Lasts. It was a dark place where Jan where no threads seemed to fully form there.

Several members of the science team were busily working at their stations. They studied Jan's brainwave telemetry. They probably hoped to discover some way of coaxing Jan to the Last of Lasts.

David peered over the back of one lab assistant's white coat. The lateral images of Jan's mind displayed orange highlights. This was where her brain was responsible for dealing with her boosted anxiety. When Threading fully began, the lateral images highlights would turn bright red and spread across the screen as if her mind was on fire.

"David, we can't delay any more. You must join the other two in the chamber," Doctor Stern said.

David was nervous. He rubbed at a metal token he kept in his pocket. He could feel the outline of a palm tree stamped on one side.

Before leaving college, he had found the token under his dorm room bed while cleaning. It was silly trinket, but for some reason he had held onto it. Maybe it continued to offer him hope. One day soon, he would find a job and pay off his college debts. Then he would have enough money to visit a tropical island, far away from the Massachusetts cold.

"David, I won't ask you to push yourself beyond your capacitive limits. That's why we've done something different with the projections today."

"Look, I don't want anyone getting hurt."

Doctor Stern made a quiet laugh. "Have you ever heard of an infinity mirror?"

"Yeah. A kind of mirror that that when you look into it, it looks like it continues on forever in the background."

"Yes. A 19th century novelty, perhaps. It's an illusion that has even been reproduced through computer simulation. But this is the year 2000. We will recreate one today through projection of light."

"I don't see how this is going to help."

The doctor tapped at David's head. David didn't like the patronizing gesture, but he said nothing.

"There are aspects of our personality that we don't even know exist. Imagine being able to explore yourself. To discover who you really are. And who you will finally be in a single moment of time," Doctor Stern said.

"So you will project an infinite image of Jan to herself. Then when she Threads, her mind will be tricked into exploring everything. Even that final place she's afraid to go. What she calls the Last of Lasts."

"Tricks are for magicians. This is science."

Trick or science, David still worried. Jan had said that if she unspooled the final thread, something bad could happen to her.

"Her mental energy conversion. What happens when the joule counter hits full capacity?"

Doctor Stern smiled as if he was speaking to a child.

"Then with the boosters, all of you could become a conduit of great power. Your minds could move mountains. Perhaps literally. Imagine the possibilities."

"And what if something else happens? What if it's not what you expect?"

Doctor Stern patted David on the shoulder. "This is science after all. We learn something new every day."

He gave David the jet injection of booster.

The chemical booster immediately made its way up David's arm like worms that crawled under his skin.

The boosted effects were different for David. He didn't suffer hyper-anxiety, like Jan. Or hallucinate, like Little Jack. Instead, David felt like he was more open to the sensations of his surroundings. Eventually his muscles would stiffen and he lost control of decision making. He also lost all sense of time.

When boosted, all David could do was *feel*. He could actually sense the mental energies of both Jan and Little Jack within his mind's eyes. It was through this concentrated brain activity that Doctor Stern hoped to convert David's mental activity to some form of physical energy.

David slowly made his way over to the Focus Chamber to join Jan and Little Jack. The booster continued to work on him.

The chamber door made a soft click behind David as an electromagnet locked him in. Vents above whispered circulated air so that the three of them could breath.

David prepared himself. He wrapped a wireless telemetry band around his forehead and wrists. Then he gripped the bio-electric transfer rail with both hands. The rail spanned the length of the chamber. It was made of highly conductive copper, a good material for the transfer of energy between the three Threaders. David could sense that it was already warmed by Jan and Little Jack's mental activity.

He faced out to watch Doctor Stern talk with someone working one of the control stations. The procedure would begin soon.

"Are you ready, David?" Doctor Stern mouthed the words from outside the chamber.

David couldn't hear the words, but he understood the meaning and nodded.

To his right, Little Jack had already slipped into a hallucinogenic and catatonic state. His hairy knuckles were locked around the bio-electric rail. Drool hung from his open mouth. He stared at the floor. David could smell the man's sweat. But the mental energy radiating from Little Jack was immediately felt across the bio-electric rail.

For experimental purposes, Little Jack was like a bobbin that a spool rested on. He served as a grounding point during the Threading. Little Jack's mind had latched onto some bit of selective memory while in his catatonic state. His mental energy felt focused and small, like a dot no bigger than the size of a pin's head. As long as David remembered this sensation, he could eventually retreat back to it to complete the experiment.

David would then communicate this sensation back to Jan. It's how he always managed to bring her back from her Threading. She would slowly wind back the threads. Then she would piece her mind back together from a splintered state. Thanks to Little Jack, David always felt a relief to know Jan would be okay.

The booster was really kicking in now.

David's mind was becoming an open conductor while Jan's breathing rapidly increased. He sensed her energy feeding into him. It entered his hands, crawled up his arm, and along his neck. He fed off of Jan's mind, absorbing her mental energy. In a way, his experimental relationship with her was parasitic. This was probably why he most disliked Threading.

The theory was that when Jan's joule counter hit full capacity, the peak energy she produced would supercharge a portion of David's brain. His brain would then be permanently altered. All thanks to Jan.

Doctor Stern couldn't actually say what the full result would be. There was speculation that David could become a walking energy detector without the need for boosters. Or he would develop the ability of rapid computation and extreme intelligence. Who knew? Doctor Stern believed that David was a vessel, ready to receive the gift of becoming something more than human. But was David ready for such a change? Was the world? And at what cost to Jan?

Beams of light were directed at the polycarbonate walls. They focused on Jan. David could only watch them through the see-through walls.

Jan's breathing accelerated even more. In-out-in-out. The condensation of her breath spread across the plastic interior wall. It partially obscured the view of a joule counter on a nearby workstation. David could just make out the joule counter climbing.

His muscles stiffened. His hands shook. The ability to make decisions dulled. Time was losing meaning. All he could do now was *feel*. David felt the bio-electric rail grow warmer, almost hot to the touch.

Mental energy was flowing in. Little Jack's focused dot was no bigger than the size of the head of a pin. At the same time, Jan's energy came at him in steady pulses. The two energies commingled as Little Jack's moved around inside it like the nucleus of an atom. As long as Little Jack's mental energy didn't overwhelm David, Jan would be okay.

The projected light beams changed.

They split into an array of colors that formed a square shape in the air. Then a smaller array appeared within the first. It repeated the same color pattern while a third shape began. It was a square within a square within a square.

The spectacle dazzled David's eyes. This patterned shape continued while forming new squares within more new squares. David lost himself, hypnotized by the barrage of shapes that seemed to go on forever.

He could feel his mind changing. It was as if the beams of lights formed a door that waited to be opened. And when it did, a multi-colored aura of energy would embrace him. It would become one with him. It wanted him to forget everything else. To forget Little Jack. To forget Jan. Just feel the door open. Feel the door. *Open it, David. Open—*

Jan whimpered. The sound broke the light's hypnotic spell over David.

He suddenly realized that Little Jack's dot of energy was disappearing from his mind. David was losing it. Its sense of existence vanished and reappeared before vanishing again. If he didn't do something fast, David would lose it altogether and Jan's mind would be lost.

Doctor Stern pointed at the joule counter and grinned at the lab assistant.

David's thoughts raced but he couldn't act. Was this what the Doctor had wanted all along? That to get through the final boundary, Jan's Last of Lasts, he must sacrifice her mind?

In David's hypnotic state, he had forgotten about Little Jack's dot of energy altogether. He would have allowed Jan to have continued threading to infinity. And with no sanctuary to return to, Jan's mind would never return from her splintered state.

Little Jack's dot faded again. Jan's whimper turned into intermittent gasping.

With no sense of time, David couldn't tell for how long this was all going on for. His own boosted state held David back. His hands shook. His stiffened muscles would not release the transfer rail. He struggled to concentrate, to make his feet move, to try and grab Jan and snap her out of her state of mind. But he couldn't get himself to act.

And even if he could shake Jan back to consciousness, would the sudden interruption permanently shatter her mind?

All David could do was *feel*. And what he felt was anger. The emotion grew within that area of his mind where Little Jack's sanctuary and Jan's splintered energy commingled.

He thought of Jan. Of how scared she must be right now. Of how Doctor Stern considered her nothing more than disposable. David's anger grew more and it overwhelmed all his thoughts.

The anger burst out. David could feel the emotional disruption leave his hands and flow outward along the transfer rail. Jan gasped and David heard her collapse to the chamber's floor.

David somehow must have forced Jan to spool back her mind.

Outside the chamber, Doctor Stern pointed at David. His brow was furrowed and his mouth turned down in anger. The joule counter was dropping. The projected lights shut down. A lab assistant rushed over and unlocked the Focus Chamber door.

David's booster effect began to wear off. His hands relaxed even though they felt somewhat heavy and stiff. This was unusual, because it usually took hours for the booster to fully work its way out of his body. He was able to release the rail and turn his head. Jan lay shaking.

Doctor Stern stood in the doorframe of the focus chamber. His face was taut. A vein stood raised on his forehead. His mouth was twisted in a look of both frustration and disgust.

"You are on the brink of greatness, David," Doctor Stern said.

David glared back. "You would have destroyed her mind."

"You short-sighted—"

David found the strength to ball his shaking hands into painful fists. He stepped forward. The doctor stood only several inches from him in the small chamber. Then he punched Doctor Stern in the nose.

Blood sprayed as the doctor stumbled back. Both hands covered his wounded face. Drops of blood fell on the floor.

The lab assistant grabbed David. He held him back from punching the doctor a second time. David was too weak to resist.

"We'll do the experiment again tomorrow. No more weeklong breaks before another Threading," Doctor Stern said. He looked over at Jan who shivered as if she were freezing cold. "I don't care if she's ready or not."

David could do nothing but watch Doctor Stern leave the experiment's control center. The lab assistant would not release him so that he could help Jan. He was forced outside the chamber as more assistants came in. They carried her out like a limp rag doll.

Little Jack still gripped the transfer rail, locked in a catatonic state. David felt just as helpless.

THAT NIGHT, David knocked at Jan's dormitory door. She didn't answer so he let himself in.

The room was dark except for one light near her bed. Clothes she had worn earlier were tossed on the floor in a crumpled pile. A discarded book lay open on the floor. David made his way over to her.

"You weren't at dinner. I brought you a piece of cake," David said.

Jan said nothing. She lay on her side in bed wearing a t-shirt and pair of shorts. Her dyed black hair was disheveled. Her back was to him and it rose and fell in slow breaths.

David could tell that the booster had worn off her. He put the small plate of cake next to the lamp that rested on a nightstand.

"Jan, are you okay?"

There was silence for a moment. "You shouldn't have stopped me today."

"What do you mean?"

"The booster's symptoms. I had more tonight. I can't take this anymore," Jan said.

"Maybe you should drop out of the program. Doctor Stern can find someone else no problem."

Jan turned over to look at him. In the pale yellow light, he could see her mascara more clearly. Dried tears had streaked her face.

She shook her head. "I don't think the side effects can be reversed. I can't live like this anymore."

David sat on the bed. "You don't mean that."

"I want to splinter my mind. Forever."

"But you were so scared in the chamber."

"I...I don't remember. Maybe I was. But I've thought about it. I want to go to the Last of Lasts and never come back."

David reached into his pocket. He pulled out the metal token with the palm tree and placed it in her hand.

"I found this just before I left college. When I start to give up hope, I rub this between my thumb and forefinger. It reminds me that there are better places in this world. This token gives me hope."

Jan's lips trembled. "I want to forget all this. Forget everything."

"There's more for you Jan. There's more outside of this lab."

Jan made a weak smile. She briefly held the metal token up to the light. The stamped palm tree glinted. She gave it back to David.

"That's sweet. But I don't think there's hope for me."

"Jan, the Last of Lasts. There's some places we probably shouldn't explore. Don't let yourself go there tomorrow."

"David?" Jan's brown eyes were wide.

"Yes?"

"Will you hold me?"

David lay beside Jan and wrapped her in his arms. She felt small and frail. She shook slightly as she cried into his chest.

"I wish I had your hope. I do," Jan said.

"Maybe together we can do something. Maybe we can cross the Last of Lasts together."

"How?"

That was the million dollar question.

Tomorrow, Doctor Stern would devise some way to ensure that David would not interrupt the experiment again. And if that happened, Jan would never stop threading. Her mind lost forever in a splintered state. And David wouldn't be there for her.

The only solution David could think of was that he should try to focus again on his anger. Somehow it had helped him to overcome his boosted state during today's experiment. The emotion had enough energy to interrupt Jan's threading.

Could he produce that kind of anger again?

Jan's breathing had quieted as she drifted off to sleep.

As David lay there, he concentrated on the image of

Doctor Stern's bloodied face. He imagined himself squeezing the image into such a tight space within his mind that it pressed together like a pill capsule under compression.

The image burst out and escape. David tried again. Over and over he worked on this until he became mentally exhausted.

He wasn't sure if the effort was useful. Hopefully, he had conditioned himself so that he would still remember where the anger resided. What else could he do? Doctor Stern had scientific training, a support staff, and advanced technology. All David had was his feelings.

David felt like an ant among giants.

THE NEXT MORNING, someone banged on David's dormitory door. When he opened it, three stone-face security guards in black uniforms walked in.

The men were abrupt. They told David to quickly change because the experiment would begin soon. They answered no questions and refused him the option of breakfast.

After he was dressed, they cuffed his hands behind his back. This was obviously a precaution to ensure that David didn't cause any more problems for Doctor Stern.

When David arrived at the TECC, Doctor Stern was already there talking with a lab assistant. His nose had stopped bleeding but a large bruise and some swelling served as a reminder of yesterday's altercation.

David smiled to himself. It was a small bit of satisfaction which made up for the uncomfortable steel handcuffs that restrained him now.

The guards ushered him over to where Little Jack stood

waiting. The short man raised his hands as if to say, "Why?" David motioned with his eyes over at Doctor Stern. Little Jack made a vulgar gesture with his middle finger at the doctor's back and then grinned. David returned the grin.

The guards must have also come for Jan. She was already in the focus chamber prepping. She had changed out of her shorts and t-shirt from the night before. But her hair was still disheveled. She hadn't cleaned off the streaked mascara from her face. And her eyes looked tired and confused.

Her breathing was accelerating as condensation built on the polycarbonate interior.

David had no way to speak to Jan. He could only hope that their time together last night had changed her mind about the Last of Lasts.

"It's good to see you cooperating, David," Doctor Stern said.

"I'm handcuffed. Do I have a choice?"

David thought again of the anger that he tried to encapsulate in his mind last night. Just like a pill capsule. Seeing Doctor Stern in the lab now only made the emotion more intense and more difficult to compress.

The Doctor picked up a needle syringe and pointed it at David. The syringe was something new.

The lab assistant nodded. Together, Doctor Stern and the assistant walked over. Doctor Stern made a smile that was probably intended to be mocking. David thought the act to be comical. A bulbous swell had spread across both the Doctor's upper lip and nose that resembled something like a purple onion.

"I don't blame you for yesterday. You were boosted. And your little act of—" The Doctor's face grew dark and red for a moment. "Your act of enthusiasm was most likely due to the temporary symptoms of dementia."

"Take these cuffs off. Let's prove your scientific theory."

Little Jack grunted a laugh and slapped at his knee.

The lab assistant used a jet injector on Little Jack's exposed arm. Little Jack grew quiet. A guard assisted him as he hobbled over to the focus chamber.

"You've had your fun, David. Now I have mine."

Doctor Stern leaned close. His breath came at David's face in hot puffs. It smelled faintly of breath mints, something the Doctor probably used to cover up the stale odor of morning coffee.

The Doctor held up the same syringe he had shown the lab assistant a minute ago. Inside it was an opaque yellow solution.

"It contains Scopolamine. Some call it truth serum. My intent is different. We'll be doing a narcosynthesis on you as a controlled intravenous hypnosis. It will enhance your booster."

The long needle burned as it entered David's arm. A few seconds later, the Doctor finished and patted him on the shoulder.

"Wouldn't want you to harm yourself during the threading, David."

"You don't care about us. Any of us. Just your results."

Doctor Stern said nothing.

A guard forced David over to the chamber. The uniformed man opened the door and unlocked the cuffs. David's body felt relaxed. He didn't resist. The syringe had already started working. When the guard told him to place his hands on the bio-electric rail, he complied without a second thought. Then the guard left the chamber and locked the door.

David felt weightless.

He looked over at Jan. Her breaths came in quick, short bursts. In-out-in-out-in-out. It was like a ticking clock. Then the sound turned into a humming bird's beating wings. David's mind jumped to the image of a butterfly as it hovered on soft breeze.

How wonderful this chamber felt. It was warm in here, embracing him like a blanket. Its protective walls kept away bad doctors and mean guards.

He wanted to say something to Jan. But he couldn't quite remember what.

"Butterfly. Okay. Little pill." That was all he could manage to say.

The little pill. Was that from last night? Was it curved and smooth and shiny? David wanted to taste it, a fragile thing upon his tongue. He envisioned bright colors swirling inside its tiny capsule. He wanted the colors to break free and fill his mouth with rainbow warmth. A pill full of rainbow colors seemed funny and this thought made David laugh.

But he grew quiet when the projected lights began. Multiple colors. Squares within squares. David watched them and thought they were beautiful.

From somewhere nearby, David could hear the sound of waves. They seemed to ebb and flow onto some distant shore. Back and forth. Back and forth.

Was that someone breathing? No. He was floating on water. Somewhere nearby there must be an island. He imagined palm trees rooted in white sand.

He remembered how much he liked palm trees. And the ocean. And islands. But he couldn't see them now because a fog spread before his eyes. He tried to reach out and wipe away the fog. His hands wouldn't cooperate.

What if he swallowed the pill? That pill full of colorful swirling lights. Would that light shine out and show him where the island was?

"I wouldn't want you to harm yourself, David." Doctor Stern's voice seemed to loom nearby. But that was impossible. David was floating in the ocean.

David imagined picking up the pill and putting it into his mouth. His arms grew warmer. Then, almost hot. Then his tongue grew hot. The heat crawled up his neck.

"You've had your fun, David."

But David wanted to bite into the pill. To taste the swirling colors as they broke free. He wanted to see the island.

The pill lay hot on his tongue. It made his brain hot. Fire hot. For a moment, he became afraid.

"David, you are just an ant. Ants cannot go to islands," Doctor Stern's voice said to him.

But ants could live on islands. It made no sense. David grew angry. Then furious.

"Wrong. Wrong, Doctor Stern."

David would prove what ants could do. He bit into the pill.

David's hypnotic spell was immediately broken.

It was like an explosion. Energy erupted from his brain. It traveled down his neck and out his hands. He couldn't stop it.

Again, another mental explosion. This time, the energy rushed out from all over his body. It was a convulsion of so much force that it caused the air to crackle and arc. The smell of plasma filled the chamber.

"Stop!" Jan screamed.

David turned his head. Jan was gripping the bio-electric rail as if she would fall from some great height.

David could see white, ethereal threads flow out and spread out from her eyes. They wavered in front of him. Then they wrapped themselves around his arms and upper body, touching him with their bristled feelers. They pulled tighter, and he knew that they could crush the life out of him.

David couldn't control his mind. The explosion happened again. His mind was on fire, a volcano that continued to erupt.

The threads responded by pulling tighter, feeding off his energy and hungry for more. They were parasites that would suck him dry.

"Release me," David said. He meant it as a command. It sounded like a plea for mercy.

The writhing threads hesitated, still hungry.

"If you don't release me, I will shut my mind off. You will starve." He wasn't actually sure he could do this but he had to try the bluff.

The threads obeyed. They pulled back and away. David began to collect his thoughts again as the threads retreated.

"David, I can't see. I'm blind," Jan said.

Jan's eyes were milky white. They were the same color as the ethereal threads that had erupted from them.

Little Jack had come out of his catatonic state. He gawked open-mouthed at something outside the chamber walls.

Doctor Stern, the lab assistants, and the uniformed guards stood in place. Doctor Stern was caught in a pose of excitedly grabbing a guards arm and pointing at the focus chamber. He appeared to be alive and frozen in time.

David's mind convulsed again. Little Jack radiated a blue field that rippled out from his body. The field spread out and covered everyone outside the focus chamber. The field must have acted as a time distortion field.

David realized that he must be like a battery for both Jan and Little Jack. He had stored and now sourced mental energy for their new abilities. Jan could emit the ethereal threads similar to what she had done during the experimental procedures. Little Jack seemed to be able to stop time or force people into a catatonic state of sorts.

But David also realized he might be able to control them to some extent.

He focused his thoughts on the chamber walls. The ethereal threads responded. They spread out in a complex pattern over its hard surface. David sensed that they weren't willing to expend any more of the precious, mental energy he supplied them. It would take someone else to force them to act into their full capacity.

"Jan, listen to me. I want you to imagine that the chamber walls are broken into a million pieces. Can you do that?"

Jan still gripped the rail. She was blind and afraid. She did nothing. David touched one of her hands. Slowly, she let go of the rail. She put her hands in his and nodded in agreement. David felt convulsions of energy flow from him and into Jan. The threads glowed.

It should have been impossible. Doctor Stern had told David that the focus chamber's walls were impact resistant enough to take a bullet. The thick polycarbonate cracked. Lines spider-webbed under the ethereal threads grip. Seconds later, the walls splintered and dropped into thousands of small pieces of plastic.

They were free.

David's mind was rapidly cooling off. He most likely spent all of his mental energy on the effort to destroy the chamber wall. The threads snaked their way back into Jan. David sensed that they waited to someday emerge and to be fed again.

He squeezed Jan's hands. She returned the squeeze. They had survived the Last of Lasts mentally intact.

"We're leaving this place," David said.

"What about Doctor Stern?" Jan said.

David looked around at the frozen men in the lab. The Doctor had never budged. Little Jack still pulsed a blue field, but it was growing dimmer.

"Little Jack's already taken care of him."

"I can't see anyone."

"I'll explain later. But we have to get going. Let's just hope that whatever Little Jack did will last until we're far away from this building."

All three of them made their way out. They stepped over pieces of broken plastic. David guided Jan as they worked their way around the time-frozen Doctor Stern and his scowling guards. The doors that lead out from TECC were only a few feet away.

The Doctor, the lab assistants and the guards never moved. David imagined Doctor Stern's frustration when he later discovered that his 'lab rats' had escaped. He grinned.

When the three of them made it out to the hallway, David could see the exit out of the building. No one tried to stop them.

"David, where are we going?" Jan said.

David reached into his pocket and fingered the metal token. He pulled it out and flipped it in the air. The token landed back in his hand. The palm tree glinted in the overhead light.

"Let's go find some hope."

Little Jack just slapped his knee and snorted a laugh.

Another blue field rippled outward from him, much fainter than the previous ones. It was something like a hiccup and it gave him the appearance of a blinking Christmas light.

Minutes later, they were outside. The sun was shining on them like a warm day on a tropical island.

WAKING FROM AN ETERNAL SLEEP

The villagers of Dinnish Pa'kor stood on the shore of the Lake of Shadows. They gathered in small groups as they quietly spoke of Dabi's murder.

Shiran did not join the others. She knew that many of the villagers were intrigued by the recent events. The great yellow suns warmed their nearly naked bodies while they nervously talked amongst themselves. They spoke of secrets. Some stole glances at Dabi's covered body that lay by the Lake's poisonous waters.

Instead, Shiran stood near Abian.

She wanted to say many words to the shackled man. He kneeled in the sand, head cast down, rough steel collars wrapped around his raw-chaffed wrists and neck. Two guards stood behind him. They held thick-handled wood shafts tipped with spearheads. These weapons were meant to cause a painful death.

But Abian said nothing.

This angered Shiran. "It will go even worse for you when you are submerged in the Lake of Shadows. In there, your body will dissolve. You will not have an eternal sleep amongst the stars."

Abian looked up at her. His hazel eyes were dull from days of captivity and hunger. Somehow, he managed a smile.

"The Unmarked Ones have secrets. I have seen them with my own eyes."

"You are a liar. A liar would kill his own brother, my husband."

"Let me show you the proof of my truth. The power that the Unmarked Ones hold over all of us will come undone."

"Again, you lie. The Unmarked Ones were sent from the stars. They guide us to eternal sleep."

Shiran turned away from Abian. She no longer wanted to look at her husband's murderer. She could only think of her own secret. She had never revealed it to her husband Dabi before his death. It was her one regret and caused great sorrow within her heart.

She walked over to Dabi's body and she prayed to the Great Judge. She prayed that her secret would reach Dabi in the stars above. She also prayed that her husband should be found worthy of the sacrifice that he had made.

Before Dabi's murder, the Unmarked One named Saluman had brought wondrous news regarding a villager by the name of Jojing. The Great Judge had chosen Jojing to be taken to the stars for eternal sleep.

Both Dabi and Abian had volunteered to escort Jojing to his final rest. At first, Saluman protested. He said that this was unusual. But he consulted with the Great Judge. A large gift of food and wine had appeared near the village that night. The Great Judge must have looked favorably on Dabi and Abian's escort.

Shiran had relished in her final moments with her husband, Dabi. In the village, there was much celebrating. And Shiran had made love to her husband for the last time. Now he lay dead on the Lake's sandy shore.

The Unmarked One named Saluman approached her. Like all Unmarked Ones, he bore no black markings above his left brow. It was known that all Unmarked Ones were sent by the Great Judge as it had been for many hundreds of generations.

"Shiran, the Great Judge will soon deliver us a new gift. I have seen it in a dream. Let us look to the stars," Saluman said.

Saluman was a wise and fair man. His visions had always proved to come true. When crops had failed, he would ask the village to pray to the Great Judge. Then he would dream. Gifts would soon appear somewhere just outside the village.

Shiran ran to him and clutched at his hand.

"Abian has returned with my husband's mutilated body."

When Abian had returned, he dragged Dabi's body behind him like some dead tree stump. Dabi's face was so brutalized that she could no longer recognize the man who once had held her in his strong arms. Her heart had broken beyond what she thought was possible.

Abian had claimed someone else had done the wicked deed. But no other witness could confirm such a tale of twisted imagination.

"Your pain must be great. But how do you know that it was Abian that killed your husband?" Saluman said.

"Because he makes a false claim."

"And what is this claim?"

"He claims that men in black clothing murdered Dabi."

"Does he have a witness or proof?"

"He has none."

Saluman looked over at Abian who was still shackled and kneeling in the sand. He seemed to study the accused man. Some of the villagers gathered near. Finally, Saluman cleared his throat and spoke.

"We must always remember that the Great Judge would never wish harm to a villager. Condemning someone to the Lake of Shadows is a serious punishment. I must be fair. I will talk to Abian, the accused."

More villagers gathered around as Saluman made his way over to Abian. Abian did not look up.

"You claim to have seen other men murder Dabi," Saluman said.

"Yes. They wore black clothing and carried weapons I did not recognize."

"And did this happen near the end of the world where the stars and land meet?"

Abian looked up. He smirked.

"There are no stars. There is only a great wall which keeps us here. The black clothed men were sure to see to that. They grabbed Jojing and chased after Dabi and me. Only I escaped."

Some of the villagers murmured. Saluman looked around and raised his hand to quiet them.

"Abian, this is a strange story you tell. There are only the stars at the end of the world. It is known that no one lives further beyond the village."

Other villagers nodded their head in agreement.

"And how is it known, Saluman? No one else has seen where the stars will meet the land. Only you say this," Abian said.

Shiran became enraged at Abian's blasphemous words.

Her husband had died at the hands of that lying madman. She screamed and charged Abian so as to beat him with her fists.

Saluman and other villagers held her back. Shiran's arms were restrained. She could not wipe at the hot tears that streaked her face.

"Abian, the trouble you cause a grieving widow," Saluman said.

Abian's voice softened. "Shiran, I hid from the black clothed men. They spoke to each other as they searched for me. They knew your secret. The one that you had not revealed. Not even to Dabi before he died."

Shiran stood in shock. She was no longer struggling, no longer crying. How could it be that Abian knew that she carried a secret? It had never been revealed to anyone else.

"Do not try to worsen Shiran's state of mind," Saluman said.

"Shiran, I will tell you your secret. Then you can judge me for yourself. Will you listen?" Abian said.

Saluman turned red-faced. "Now you are being cruel to her. How can you do this?" Saluman said.

"Shiran, search your heart. You know I would never harm my brother. I have always loved him. That is why I went with him on escort. I wanted to protect him. The only thing I am guilty of is not saving his life."

"Perhaps you wished to have Shiran for yourself. In *your* heart, you believed that you could make Shiran your wife," Saluman said.

Saluman's face continued to grow redder as he yelled out the words. Shiran was surprised by the Unmarked One's anger. She had never seen him this way.

"And would I have brought my brother's body back for everyone in the village to see? Why not just hide it? I could claim that Dabi had also had walked off into the stars," Abian said.

The villagers agreed that this was reasonable.

Shiran also agreed even though this went against her feelings in her heart. She was curious. Did Abian really know her secret? This could be a test of truth to prove that proved that Abian lied. He should at least be allowed to reveal it before being tossed into the Lake of Shadows and dissolved into silence. Then Shiran's conscious would be cleared.

"I think I will pass my judgement now. It seems obvious that this man cannot be trusted," Saluman said.

Shiran held her hand up. "Wait. I want to hear what Abian will say. Tell me, Abian. What is my secret?"

Abian paused. "As the black-dressed men searched for me, they said that you were pregnant. They knew Dabi was the father. They could not allow you to give birth inside the village."

The other villagers stood silent. They looked at Shiran.

She stared at Abian. New tears streamed down her face. How could he know? Finally, she nodded.

"It is true," she said, "I am pregnant with Dabi's child."

When the crowd heard this, they yelled out that Abian had the visions of the Unmarked Ones. The Great Judge had spoken through him.

"This is madness. Impossible. He is not Unmarked. Quickly! Take Abian to the Lake of Shadows," Saluman demanded.

The villagers chanted, "Let Abian speak. Let Abian speak." They pressed in closer and surrounded Saluman. The guards looked nervously around.

Shiran walked over to Abian and touched his face.

Saluman attempted to grab Shiran and stop her. The villagers turned on him and held him back.

"If you are not the one, do you have any proof of my husband's murderer?" she said.

"My hands are shackled. Reach into my pants pocket. I have killed one of the black-dressed men and taken a trophy from him."

When Shiran pulled her hand out of Abian's pocket, she held a small, metal disk with a red jewel. The disk was cool to the touch. The red jewel pulsed. Strange symbols were etched across its golden surface.

The circular disk felt alien to her. Could it have come from the stars above? But if so, why did it cause a revulsion within her belly? This was an object that held its own secret. And this secret was greater than her own.

"The black-dressed man I killed wore that on his shirt," Abian said.

Shiran turned on Saluman. "Why would the Great Judge send others to harm Dabi? He was innocent." She spoke loudly so that all the villagers could hear her.

Abian interrupted. "Because Saluman has lied to all of us. I will take you to the black-dressed man's body. There, you will see one of the murderers."

Shiran held the metal disk up to the sunlight for the other villagers to see. It changed colors in the light, turning green and then blue and then back to a golden yellow. Some reached out to touch the alien object. Each time, their hand quickly retreated.

"Abian has shown me proof. Release him. I no longer seek an ill-gained justice," Shiran said.

The villagers agreed. The two guards removed Abian's shackles. He rubbed at his wrists and neck. Then he smiled.

"Your husband shall have his justice. I will take you to the proof."

Saluman shouted obscenities at the crowd. He told them that they were fools. That the Great Judge must have had a reason for killing Dabi. That Abian was just as guilty. And perhaps even Shiran conspired with them in a sinful way.

The two guards grabbed Saluman. They dragged him along as the villagers followed Abian and Shiran. The two of them walked side-by-side.

Shiran travelled west with Abian. They passed by the Lake of Shadows, through a woods and then into a clearing. The sun began to lower. Blue sky changed to streaks of orange and pale white of the late afternoon.

No one spoke as they walked except for Saluman. He frequently warned that the Great Judge would be angry at the villagers for treating an Unmarked One so poorly. Saluman behaved in such a way that he no longer appeared to be the wise man that Shiran had once believed him to be.

Near dusk, Abian pointed out a small cave. Its mouth was just barely visible in a large hill covered in thick, green grass.

Many of the villagers suddenly became nervous. They scratched at themselves or restrained one another. They seemed afraid that they were near the entrance to where the stars met land.

Even Shiran worried that they could violate a sacred space set aside by the Great Judge. But she did not see any stars or anything else unusual peeking out from the dark mouth of the cave. Still, she held back.

"Do not worry, Shiran. I will go into the cave. I will soon return with proof," Abian said.

Shiran watched him disappear inside. Her thoughts

turned to the alien disk Abian had showed her. How could a black-dressed man be so different from herself and the other villagers? How had recent events caused Abian to doubt the Great Judge and the eternal sleep in the stars?

"This will end badly for you all," Saluman said.

He glared at Shiran. Spittle had gathered around his mouth from yelling and constant complaining. She said nothing.

When Abian reappeared, the crowd stirred and craned their necks. Shiran stepped forward. Her curiosity overcame any fears that she might have.

Abian dragged behind him the body of what looked like a man. He wore a black shirt and pants. White stripes ran across the shoulders and down the legs. A wide belt wrapped around his waist. The belt held cylindrical shaped objects in leather loops. One object in particular puzzled Shiran. It was a long metal rod attached to a grip, a grip for a knife or a tool.

On closer inspection, she saw other things that made this black-dressed man different. He was taller than any villager by at least a full head. On top of his bloodied skull were many strands of fiber that looked like brown string. Like all the other villagers, Shiran's head was smooth and naked. When she touched the brown strings, their soft threads shifted and exposed two fleshy objects. They stuck out at both sides of the black-clothed man's head.

Shiran touched the sides of her own head. She only had two holes which were covered by a stiff, brown membrane.

"Shiran, look at his face," Abian said.

His eyes were blue like the sky above. They stared at nothing, vacant of life. *He is missing something. But what?* Then she realized that the black-clothed man had no markings above his left brow.

"He is unmarked like Saluman," Shiran said.

"These unmarked men live behind a wall north of here. They took Jojing there. But I do not know why."

"How did they kill my husband?"

Abian nodded at the long metal rod on the black-clothed man's belt. "One of them had pointed it at him. There was a loud sound like thunder. Then Dabi fell dead."

Furious, Shiran snatched the metal rod from the belt. It felt heavy and cold in her hands. The rod's grip was rough with a textured pattern. She marched over to Saluman and pointed the rod at him.

"Is this how I use it, Saluman? Do I name the person I wish to kill and point this? Tell me. Why are you unmarked? What secrets do you carry inside you?"

Saluman's eyes were wide with fear.

"Please, don't point the gun at me. If you put it down, I'll tell you what I know."

"This gun must have great power. If you do not tell me, you will be dead like Dabi."

Saluman flinched when Shiran moved her hand. But she gave the gun to Abian instead. Then she held up the metal disk.

"What is this object?"

"It's an identification badge. All uniformed security wear them."

"You know so much about the black-clothed men. Who are you really?"

"We're from a planet very far away from here. It's called Earth. It's beyond the stars you see. You call us men but we're not the same race. We are humans."

"Then why are you here?"

"To study you. Sometimes we perform experiments. That's why you've been tagged with the brow markings."

Shiran struggled to understand Saluman's words. She did not know what an *experiment* was. Or how villagers could live beyond the stars. She shook her head in confusion.

"Yet you look like us. Not like the black-dressed man. Your head is naked. Is this—"

"I was altered to look like you. For years, we have walked among you. We guide your primitive culture. We form your beliefs."

"And so the Great Judge has been planted in our heads like the food we grow? He is only a story that you and other humans have made up?"

Saluman nodded.

The other villagers were troubled by this. They asked questions amongst
themselves.

"We should kill him, Shiran. To punish Saluman for what he has done to Dabi and all of us," Abian said.

Shiran rubbed at her pregnant belly. The villagers now knew that they had been deceived. The humans would soon know, too. She feared that more humans in the stars would soon come for her child.

Even if the village were to take a stand, they would be no match against more human guns. They would all be massacred. Their best chance was to retreat, to hide, and to warn other villages.

It would not be easy to convince them. They must take the alien metal disk and the human gun with them as proof. It was their best chance. Perhaps there would come a day when the village of Dinnish Pa'kor and others united to push back the human invaders. And maybe her unborn child would lead them all to a day of freedom, a day of no experiments.

"Let Saluman go. He will send a message back to the other humans."

Abian protested. The other villagers looked shocked.

"We must be wise. There is no Great Judge that we can rely on to guide us with false words. If we kill Saluman, the humans will come for us that much sooner. We must unite with other villages and prepare. Only then will we be ready for them."

Abian walked over to Shiran to give her the gun.

"No, you must learn to use this. And we must teach others. You will become our first soldier."

Then Shiran turned to Saluman.

"I want you to take a message back to the humans."

The guards released Saluman's hands. He wiped at spittle from his mouth but he did not become aggressive.

"What would you have me say?"

"That we know about the humans. And soon all the other villages will too. If you do not leave our planet, we will someday hunt you down. And then we will come for you in the stars and hunt you at your very own Earth."

Saluman shook his head. "I will tell them. But you have too many generations to evolve for that."

"And today is the first day that we wake from our sleep in the stars."

Abian commanded Saluman to leave or there would be consequences. He pointed the gun at him. The other villagers watched the human shamble off, mumbling to himself.

Shiran turned to walk away. She waved at her people to follow. They followed.

Two moons had formed above in the darkening sky. Shiran tried to imagine life beyond the moons. What would it be like to visit places somewhere beyond the stars? A place where there were no secrets. They were not places where people told stories of Great Judges. They were places of new beginnings.

This would be a future that was made by her hands and the other villagers. No Great Judge. No Unmarked Ones. No secrets. This was a time that she had finally woken from a near-eternal sleep.

JUMP TRAINS AND SIMULTANEITY

The Chicago VI Jump Station is a lively place. All those butter-and-egg men in a rush to go somewhere. The newspaper vendors barking out the headliners of stuff I don't understand or want to know about. Coffee shops slinging fresh ground bean and sizzled bacon breakfast plates. All day, they're ringing up sales from other people who got money to spare. Ka-ching! Ka-ching! Ka-ching!

I bet it's busy just like any jump station at any space city. I could probably visit the cities Chicago II, III, or IV, then make tracks for New York XVI somewhere in the Nebulous Rim at the far edge of the Oberon Galaxy. And at each city's station, I'd probably see more butter-and-egg-men in fancy suits, more newspaper vendors and more coffee shops.

And then there would be me. A thirteen-year-old boy who carries around a box of colored shoe polishes. It's funny. Even if I could afford a ticket to ride a jump train, I probably wouldn't feel like I belong to any of those places anyway.

"Ain't it exciting, Susie? Another jump train's coming in soon," I says.

I still can't help getting worked up. A jump train arrival, that experience always makes me feel...it makes me feel like I might one day find a home. Except I don't know where home is.

Susie is getting herself ready. She hitches up the garters on her long legs. Then straightens out the cigarette packs on a tray that hang from her slender neck by a red strap. She does all that while popping her chewing gum.

"Yeah? Well, you better keep your eyes on those shoes before the polish dries, shoeshine boy."

My brush starts working fast over my customer's oxfords. A deep, warm smell tells me I'm heating up the polish just right. With enough speed and friction, I'll make them shine like new copper pennies.

"That's why I like you, Susie. You keep me honest."

"You better hope I don't get rich selling cigarettes, Bobby-boy."

"You'd miss me."

She just smirks, giving me the high hat before strutting on. From my crouched point of view, all I can see going is a black saloon skirt and those beautiful movin' uprights.

The customer pays, and I do a quick cloth rub which earns me a tip. The dropped coins rattle a nearby tin cup. My dog, a wrinkly basset hound named Mister Pleats, gives a half-hearted wag of thanks before closing his eyes again.

It's 10am. The station energy systems are about fully charged up. The jump train is coming real soon.

I once asked Tom how they work—he's one of three station conductors. Jump trains are faster-than-light machines. So at both the Departing and Arriving Stations, they have powerful computers and energy systems. Both computers are syncopated—or synchronized or synco-some-thing—to mash out some numbers for what Tom called, "An agreed upon singular coordinate in time and space."

"Yeah, what's so great about that?" I says.

"Because it's the numbers that shape the same energy field at both stations. The numbers create two places in space that a jump train exists in simultaneously," Tom says.

A Joe like me, that kind of thing makes my mouth drop.

"Oh, it gets even better," Tom says, thumbs tucked into his vest pockets.

"How's that?" I says.

"It's the computer on the jump train that has to finally resolve the differences between the two locations *actual* coordinates. That's how a train arrives."

I can't say I understood it all. But the idea that I could be in two places at once makes me wonder if I'm not really sitting on my dead Mother's lap. She's rockin' me to sleep as says that me and Mister Pleats' life is gonna' turn out just swell.

It's 10:02 on the big station clock, and the station energy systems are ready to go. You can almost sense it, like the air's gone thick and heavy-like. Even all the butter-and-egg men know it 'cause they're grinning at the station tracks like some Joe who ain't never seen a Christmas tree.

The place goes stone silent. Even if you tried to speak, no words seem to come out of your mouth. I'm smearing a dab of black paste onto a cloth, but I don't feel like I'm really movin'. Maybe I'm not. I can see the train flickering. A ghost machine jumps into several places on the track. Finally, it turns solid and stands quietly in place.

"10:02am. Arrival from Philadelphia Seven," Tom yells out over the crowd.

Lots of people are getting off. All kinds of suits. Grandparents meeting up with their families. Some scrubs coming out here for the University inside the city.

I'm looking around for a couple of shoe customers, calling out, "Shine your shoes! Shoe's shined here!" as loud as I can. Mister Pleats musters up a yelp or two to help out.

Then I see him comin' right at me. He's grinning, his black eyes shining under a pile of oiled hair. There's a buttoned double-breasted, grey suit hanging on his tall frame, and the patterned green lines that run up and down don't seem to want to be there. And he's swinging a gold pocket watch chain like he owns the place.

Hanging on his right arm is a real tomato. Wavy brown hair down to her creamy shoulders, she's all baby blues and cherry red lips that seem like they want to taste inside your soul.

"If I can see the reflection of a Methane pulse drive in those boots, there's an extra tip in it for you," the strange man says to me. He casually rests his boot on my box's stand.

The tomato pinches his cheek with long, slender fingers. "Silly, you know there's no such thing."

"And that's what they said about humans."

I hop to it, pretending not to listen to those two bumping gums. I quickly start working any dirt and mud off the strange man's boots, my second brush primed to make those boots glow, if that's what it takes.

I look over to see Mister Pleats in the tomato's arms. He's belly up to her like a baby and pawing playfully. He practically oozes when she scratches his chin and tells him that he's the cutest specimen she's ever seen.

"I found him when he was just a puppy. Nobody wanted him. I gave him a bite of my ham sandwich, and we've been friends since," I says.

"Do you have any other friends?" the strange man says.

"Nope. Just me and Mister Pleats."

The strange man studies me. I try not to notice.

"No family? No one else in this city?" he says.

"I sleep under a tarp near the loading bay, if you must know mister. Say, you ain't a cinder dick are you?"

"I'm sorry—a what?"

"A copper. They work the station undercover."

"Do I dress like one?"

I glance around. I see Freckles and a few other of Charlie Hands' street boys loitering nearby. They act like they're just talking, but I know better. They're watching me.

You see, they first wanted me to join their gang because I don't have any family. Said they'd look after me if I gave them a cut of my shoeshines. But I know what always happens to them. They eventually wind up in the hoosegow or get the final kiss off. I told them to take a walk. So now they're wanting to muscle me out of the Station.

"I ain't a stool pigeon, mister."

The strange man thumbs back at Freckles without even turning around, like he's got eyes in the back of his head. Freckles seems to notice.

"You know, you don't have to be afraid of those guys if you don't want to be," the strange man says.

"I said I ain't no stool pigeon."

"No indeed. Just a little mouse in a never-ending maze."

I don't like what he says, but I keep my mouth shut. The polish on the second boot gets so worked up, that even I'm impressed by the rich, black color. I finish up by quickly buffing it out.

The strange man smiles at me and unfolds a bill—it's a whole sawbuck! No one's ever paid me that much for a shine. Then he shoves a business card in my hand and winks.

"I could use an apprentice. And maybe you could use a new career."

The tomato puts Mister Pleats down, and the two stroll off, arm in arm. The strange man is still swinging his pocket watch chain in the other hand.

I look over the business card as they walk away. It's all white except for three words in gold lettering: *Theodore Rattletrap, Xenoarchaeologist.*

When I look up, Freckles is looking at me with this nasty grin, nodding like he knows something I don't.

I DIDN'T THINK I had seen the last of Freckles. And I was right.

It's One pm. I buy myself a bag lunch over at Danny's Coffee Shop and something else for Mister Pleats. He wags his tail at me, and we both sit down somewhere out of the way on the walkway to eat. Danny can really pack a nice lunch, but his costs more because he's in the busiest part of the station. But after buying the two lunches and a cup of soda, I still have enough cash to finally buy Mister Pleats a small bed for him to sleep on at night.

I've finished my ham sandwich and about to bite into an apple when I see Freckles. He's casually walking over to me, hands in his overalls and whistling. He's alone, just trying to look like he's on the level, but he's as real as a greasy sourdough twenty.

Freckles earned his nickname because he's got so many of them that they practically cover him in one big blot. He's got red hair and little pink-rimmed eyes that bulge out. And his upturned nose and buckteeth make him look like a rabbit—a mean rabbit.

"Bobby-boy, slip me five." Freckles holds his hand out to me, but I just ignore him.

"I told you I'm not joining."

Freckles oozes up and puts his arm around me. He smells like salami and onions, a walking pile of stinky cold cut.

"Look, we're pals, so I'll be straight up with you. I saw that guy give you the sawbuck, so I'm gonna' cut you a deal. You give me the rest of the money, and I'll tell the boys to leave you alone for a whole month. What do you say?"

"I spent it all."

"You know it's just sitting in your pocket. I followed you around."

"Then you must know I bought a train ticket to Scram City, population you."

Freckles just laughs and pulls his arm around me tighter. It's starting to hurt. I try squirming out of his grip, but he's got me locked down.

"Aww, nuts!" I say.

"What was that, Bobby-boy?"

"Nuts!"

"I guess I'm just too nice. And I was trying to be friendly."

He's practically crushing me now. His smile turns downward into a leer. He's about to do something, just not sure if it's a punch to the gut or if he's got a knife.

I do the only thing I can think of. I reach up and smash the apple in his face. Chunks of red and white splatter everywhere.

Freckles lets go of me. He's cursing and wiping his eyes.

Finally, he looks at me, red faced. A very angry rabbit

now. I think he's gonna' charge. I brace myself, when Mister Pleats comes to my rescue. He clamps down on Freckles ankle, and the greaseball lets out a yowl.

"Get him off! Get him off!"

He's hopping about and trying to shake Mister Pleats off at the same time. With his lanky arms flapping about, Freckles is doing a discombobulated Charleston dance. Other people take notice, and they slow down to point and laugh. He looks ridiculous, and I can't help but laugh too. But I kind of feel bad for him, too.

"Mister Pleats, come here boy."

Mister Pleats lets go, wags his tail at me, and waddles over. I give him a scratch on the head.

"You're gonna' give me that money, Bobby-boy. And pay extra."

I look down at Freckle's pant leg, which is torn and tattered where he got bit. He's got teeth marks and small puncture wounds with only a little bit of blood. But he'd be all right.

"Tell Charlie Hands hello for me," I says.

Freckles is limping away. His face is still red, still the mean rabbit. "I know where you sleep, Bobby-boy."

FRECKLES STILL WORRIED ME. Mister Pleats bit him and he wouldn't forget that. And he wouldn't forget the money or the apple I smashed in his face.

At 3pm, the city dog catcher starts snoopin' around the station. Then he spots me and Mister Pleats and comes over.

I knew who made the call—Freckles. The dog catcher wouldn't actually say who called about Mister Pleats. But he said he couldn't allow a dog with no license to be on the streets. I told the dog catcher what happened with Freckles and that Mister Pleats was just tryin' to help.

"Can't afford to be partial. It's a matter of protecting the public health," he says and rubs at his bristly mustache. Then he snatches up Mister Pleats like he was a wild bobcat or something, shovels him into the back of his hover truck, and drives off.

I feel like the Chicago Trade Building had just collapsed on my head. The only thing I can do is flatfoot it out to the Pound on West Madison Street and Monroe. So I hide my shoeshine box beneath the tarp I sleep under, and hope I can get Mister Pleats out of the hoosegow.

The Pound is about fifteen blocks away. I'm running past people—some who are yelling at me—"Watch where you're going, buddy."—but I keep on rushing. Several more street crossings, a cut through an alley, and I get there at about a quarter to four. Fortunately, the place doesn't close until six.

It's an ugly, squat building. Sad red brick that's faded by too much dirt and time. Only one small window facing out. And there's a heavy front door that's rusted orange at the hinges.

When I enter through the door, the inside isn't much better. The overhead light above the front desk paints the room phlegm yellow. It smells stale in here, like hardly anyone ever comes here. There's a receptionist, her short blond hair hanging down near her eyes as she works a file over her nails. It's a rough, scratchy sound—krrrrruck, krrrrruck. She doesn't even bother to look at me when the door chime announces my arrival.

I've got about eight-fifty in my pocket, and it better be enough.

"Hi," I says.

She just keeps filing her nails. I raise my voice.

"I'm here to pick up Mister Pleats. How much is it? I ain't got all day."

The receptionist still doesn't look at me. "I don't know any Mister Pleats."

"The dog catcher picked him up a couple of hours ago."

She huffs through her nose, puts down the file, and picks up a clipboard.

"A basset hound?"

I get excited. "That's him."

I pull out my money from my pocket, a wad of crumpled bills and some change.

"It's thirty-five, kid."

"What? That ain't right."

"Twenty-five for the impound fee. Ten for a new license. I don't make the rules."

She goes back to her nails. Krrrrruck. Krrrrruck.

My mind is spinning faster than a loop-the-loop. I'd be lucky to make a couple bucks in a day, but I still got to pay for food and stuff. What if it took a month to save the thirty-five? Two months?

"What happens to Mister Pleats if I take too long to get you the dough?"

"You don't want to know, kid."

Just then, the door chime announces someone else behind me. The receptionist jerks up straight in her chair, drops the file, straightens out her hair, and smiles. Yeah, she actually cracks a smile.

"Hello little mouse," a man says.

I turn to see Theodore Rattletrap and his tomato standing there. Same pile of oiled hair, same double-breasted suit, and that gold watch chain he likes to swing around. The receptionist is making whoopee-eyes at him, totally ignoring the tomato.

Rattletrap turns to her. "I was looking for a basset hound. I hear that they're an amazing specimen of what you call 'dogs.'"

The receptionist still can't take her eyes off him. "You are so lucky. One just came in. I'd be happy to show you."

"Thank you. You are the loveliest creature.'

She lets out a strained laugh that sounds like a tommy gun—ha-uh-ha-uh-ha. Then she scoops up a keycard. Rattletrap isn't even looking at me, so I'm about to say something. But the receptionist opens the door that leads back to kennel before I can get a word out. I tag along.

The dog cages are stacked two high and run along both the left and right. A lot of them have mutts inside, and they perk up when we walk by, hoping we're going to notice them.

When we get toward the end of the row, the tomato lets out a squeal of delight. That's when I see Mister Pleats at the back wall. At first he's looking kind of sad, his chin flopped down on his front paws. But he sits up, wags his tail, and gives out a deep-throated bark to let me know he's okay.

The Tomato runs her slender finger across Rattetrap's chin. "Can I have him, Teddy? He's so cute."

"This is the one. We'll take him," Rattletrap says.

The receptionist doesn't even mention the thirty-five, probably thinking Rattletrap is loaded with dough or something. She says she's going to get some paperwork and that she'll be right back.

"I'm already missing you," Rattletrap says.

The receptionist's mouth drops and she goes all goo-goo like. Then she kind of fumbles backward as she makes her way out, all the time Rattletrap is making cutesy waving gestures at her.

"Rattletrap, what are you trying to do to Mister Pleats?"

"He's my dog now, little mouse. Maybe I'll change his name."

I'm getting mad, and I can feel my legs and arms shaking. I feel like I want to cry, and I'm wiping at my eyes so I don't look like a baby.

"You're going to xeno…xenogist him, aren't you?"

Rattletrap laughs.

"I'm a xenoarchaeologist, not some human taxidermist. Do you even know what a xenoarchaeologist is?"

The tears are starting to flow now, and I can't stop them, big blobs of wet. I still remember the first day I gave Mister Pleats a bite of my ham sandwich. I shake my head.

"I study alien life forms. Like you. And Mister Pleats. I find your kind totally fascinating. But I promise you that I mean you no harm."

Rattletrap isn't making any sense. There's space cities all over the Oberon Galaxy. Jump trains coming and going from the Chicago VI Station all the time. And I've never seen little green men getting off a train, antennas poking out of their round heads as they chirp out strange words like excited birds.

"There's no such things as aliens, mister."

Rattletrap smiles.

"That's what we've said about you. Our councils thought you were a mythical creature until humans began spreading further out amongst the stars."

"You're just saying that stuff because you think I'm some dumb kid."

"I have no reason to lie."

The receptionist returns with some paperwork. She

hands it to Rattletrap with another tommy gun laugh. Then she opens Mister Pleats cage, imprints his license number on one of his ears, and scans it to make sure it takes.

"He's all yours, Mister..."

"Rattletrap. Theodore Rattletrap."

"That's such a nice name. Can I call you Teddy?"

"You can call me most anything you want, just don't call me naughty."

Again, the tommy gun laugh—ha-uh-ha-uh-ha.

"I'll be sure to remember it so I can update your paperwork."

The Tomato squeals again as she takes Mister Pleats in her arms. He's pawing at her playfully, not even bothering to look at me. I start crying again.

"Mister Pleats, don't you miss your pal?" I says.

"You. Move along. Don't bother these nice people," the receptionist says.

Rattletrap and the Tomato are walking out of the kennel, Mister Pleats in the Tomato's arms. I don't know what to say or do. Then Rattletrap turns back to me.

"You still have my card, don't you little mouse?"

"Yes," I manage to blubber out.

"Then come work for me. Be my apprentice."

"Will you give me back Mister Pleats?"

Rattletrap doesn't say anything as he's about to leave with my dog.

"Where do I find you, mister? Where do I find you?"

"You will. You just will," Rattletrap calls back.

I'M SITTING ON A BENCH, back at the station, and the place just isn't the same. At 9pm, I'm usually packing up my shoeshine box, counting my money, and then I go see if Danny's got any left overs for me and Mister Pleats. But I'm just sitting there on that bench, alone, not even bothering to go over Danny's. I watch the night sweepers pushing away garbage with their bristled brooms. I feel no better than a crumb that gets swept away into a bag. A real crumb.

Susie must have finished her shift because she doesn't have the cigarette tray strapped around her neck. She's walking my way, but I don't even bother to look at her gartered legs. I don't feel like talking.

"Hey Bobby-boy. Hey, I'm talkin' to you."

"Yeah?"

She pops her chewing gum.

"Some friends of yours were looking for you. They said they got something for you."

I sit straight up. The only person who'd be looking for me is Freckles. He wants revenge for when I smashed that apple in his face. Made him look like a twit in front of a bunch of strangers. And some of Charlie Hands' street boys would make sure that I wouldn't be smashing a second apple. My night is about to get worse. Much worse.

"Geez. You should have told him to take a long walk on a short pier."

Susie puts her hands on her hips. "Bobby, don't be rude with me."

"Sorry. I'm just a little glum."

"What's a shoeshine kid got to be glum about?"

That makes me pretty mad. I want to yell at her.

"Yeah, what do you know? Nothin', that's what. You know nothin'."

"Geez, Bobby, you'd think you'd lost your best friend or something." Then she walks off in a huff, like I'm the one insulting her.

I want to say more, but I spy out Freckles searching around an empty ticket station further down. He's out here at the station's closing time because he knows that no one is going to be around to help me.

I've got to find some place to hide. I can't go back to Loading 'cause Freckles has already told me that he knows I sleep there. The only place I can think of is cargo storage. It's several levels high with stairs and elevators, and I might be able to slip into one of the units to hide behind stacked boxes.

As quietly as I can, I sneak off toward the back end of the station.

I have to creep alongside the hovering tracks because there's less light here. Just to my left is the open space of where the jump trains appear. Living in a city that exists literally in space, you eventually come to a place where the concrete stops and a deep plunge into cold vacuum happens. The only thing between everyone who lives in Chicago VI and a quick death is some sort of energy shield that protects us all. But that hasn't stopped a few crumb-bums from taking their own lives by taking a leap over some guard railing. That's not going to be me.

I can see the first set of stairs leading up to storage. My feet are clanking on the steel steps. Below, I can hear someone say that they hear something. I grab another cold handrail and continue on.

The first unit's door is locked. I jiggle at it, trying to not make any noise. There's a window, but it won't slide open. I can see boxes stacked inside. If I were to break the window, someone would hear that for sure. I go up more flights.

Two more units and still no luck. This situation is throwing me a curve. It's when I get to the fourth level one that I finally get a break. The window is cracked open because someone forgot to close it. I pull myself up and flop over to the other side. I bang my arm up a little as I land, but that's nothing compared to what Freckles will do to me if he catches me.

Then I lock the window closed from the inside and hope for the best.

It's dusty in here, small bits of stuff floating all around tied rolls marked *Cotton Batting* and some sort of insulation. Maybe that's why someone opened the window. It makes me want to cough, but I cover my mouth when I hear clanking footsteps coming up.

"Bobby-boy, you up here?"

It's Freckles, and he's just a level below me. Someone plays at the unit's door, testing it. Then several footsteps come up to where I'm at. I slink down in a couple of rolls of cotton.

"Bobby, I found your shoeshine box."

They test the door which doesn't budge. I can see someone peeking into the window, their beady eyes scanning around. I try to get even lower when my nose starts to twitch. I want to sneeze.

"Your shoeshine box is in little itty-bitty pieces, all over the station."

Some of the boys laugh. I'm desperately fighting back the sneeze. My eyes are starting to water.

"You got nothing left, Bobby-boy. So come out."

Freckles gets quiet for a moment, listening. I'm pinching my nose, holding back the sneeze. I don't know how much more of this I can take. Fortunately, he gets tired of not hearing anything and decides to move on.

I'm holding my breath to stop myself from exploding out of my nose and I'm starting to get a headache. A minute goes by. I take a few cautious breaths. Then a few more minutes pass. Finally, the urge to sneeze passes.

I must have waited about an hour. I don't hear Freckles and the boys anymore. I sneak a peak out the window. Only empty stairs. I start to cough, getting all this dust out of my lungs—it's almost like a spasm. Then I calm myself. I listen. Nothing. No one noticed.

I really want to get out of this dust box, so I open the window again and crawl out. I land with a thud on steel platform. I hold my breath, but I still don't hear anything. Maybe Freckles got tired of searching for me. I don't think it's true. If there's any quality I can pin on him besides being mean, it's that he's really stubborn.

I look around. Then down. The coast is clear.

My luck seems to have changed for the better.

Going slower, supporting my weight on the handrails, the steel steps clank is muffled as I make my way back down. No one shouts out. Third level. Second level. Almost back on the station platform, when murmurs carry somewhere from behind me, the storage units three rows down.

So much for luck. I'll have to make my way back along the station tracks, get to the main entrance, and escape into the city.

I'm creeping along the hovering tracks, again, but this time in reverse. There's columns every ten feet, so I get to another one, press myself against it, and scan ahead for trouble. I'm moving pretty slow. It's better to be cautious.

It's when I get to the thirteenth column—yeah, lucky number thirteen—when I freeze. Ahead, a group of Charlie Hands' boys are loitering in a group, smoking cigarettes, and telling dirty jokes. They don't see me. The murmuring that I heard earlier is coming from behind, and it's getting closer. I'm trapped. My odds of just sneaking by the boys without being seen aren't good. I'm thinking about making a run past them and hoping for the best.

"Psst. Little mouse. Over here."

Goosebumps are crawling up my arm and neck. It's definitely Rattletrap's voice. But I don't see anyone.

"The tracks. I want you to jump," Rattletrap says.

"You some kind of genius? I'll fall and die."

"No you won't. I promise."

Suddenly, Rattletrap's face appears in mid-air over the tracks. He's grinning at me. I almost yell out like I've just seen a ghost, but manage to control myself.

"You don't have much time. Jump the guard rail now."

Then his grinning face disappears again.

The murmurs are getting closer. I don't have much time. Rattletrap is right.

I make a break for the guard rail. My breath is sucked in. I will all the strength in my legs that I can manage.

I run right at the rail which is about three feet high, plant my hands, and vault over.

My eyes are closed. If I'm going to fall into space, I don't want to see it.

Someone yells out, "Hey, did you see that?"

"Yeah, I think someone's over there," someone else says.

I'm waiting to free fall. But I don't.

I can feel solid floor underneath my feet. My shoes shuffle on something that might be a knit rug of some kind as I regain my balance. I hear the soft tick of a nearby clock and a throat clearing. Odors of old paper, cedar and leather are filling my nose. The smells and sounds reminds me of the downtown library for some reason. It's where I sometimes go to hide away from my troubles and get lost in an adventure book. It's a place I can feel safe for a bit.

When I open my eyes, I'm standing in a strange room

that seems to hover in space. Books cover one wall from top to bottom. Yellowed charts and diagrams, hundreds of them, cover another wall painted red. Pinned collages of unreadable figures and sketches are everywhere. There's two lounge chairs with a small table between them, the legs made of sculpted metal to look like lions.

Rattletrap is sitting on one of the lounge chairs and the Tomato is in another. She has Mister Pleats on her lap. As soon as I sees him, he wags his tail and barks.

"Isn't the control of simultaneity a marvel?" Rattletrap says.

I shake my head. I have no idea what he's talking about.

"Where are we?"

Rattletrap is studying his pocket watch, the protective flap open. "We're in a different inertial frame of reference. A room within another space and time. As far as your friends out there are concerned, we don't exist. Very complex stuff."

I turn and see Freckles and the boys scratching their head just several feet away. But they can't see me.

"So, am I trapped in here or something?"

"On the contrary. The galaxy has now opened up to you."

"I can travel without a jump train?"

"Little mouse, you do ask a lot of questions. I'll explain a little, for a little is all I still know about humans. After your great wars on Earth, humans thought it best to span out through various galaxies. Spreads out the risk of another incident, I suppose. It's also why your leaders limit your access to technology. Only approved operators are allowed the limited secrets humans possess. Can't have everyone learning too much, doing too much. That goes for jump trains, too."

The Tomato gets up and brings Mister Pleats over to me. He's wiggling with excitement and practically jumps into my arms.

"Thank you. I've missed him. But I still don't understand any of this."

"Let's take a ride," Rattletrap says.

He does something on his pocket watch. Suddenly we're standing in a jump train car. There's only one other person here, a man reading a newspaper. The headlines are dated for yesterday. He doesn't see us.

Then we appear in another car. Or maybe it's another jump train because the windows have different colored curtains. There's a family here, a father, mother, and a boy. The father is smoking a pipe. The warm cherry tobacco smell makes me think that this is how all father's smell. The boy is reading a comic book, and his mother is stroking his wavy hair. I want to be in that boy's place, letting his mother comfort me, telling me that I don't have to shine shoes anymore.

"I feel like I'm home," I says.

"In a galaxy so vast, what really is home?"

And now we jump again. I'm surrounded by stars and darkness. It seems to go on forever. I suddenly feel tiny, insignificant. Freckles is far, far away. I don't even care anymore. There is so much more out here than shoe shine boxes and a jump train station.

"What do you think of all of this?" Rattletrap says.

"Like I could find a family some day."

Rattletrap smiles at me. He puts his hand on my shoulder.

I'm still taking in all the stars that surround me. Small ones, bright ones, blue ones. Thousands of them. And further on, thousands more. I feel good inside, just like I ate the best ham sandwich in all of Chicago VI.

"It's only your imagination that will limit you, little mouse."

"I want to be your apprentice. I want to be a Xeno...Xeno..."

Rattletrap smiles again. "You have much to learn before I can call you anything."

The stars all seem to say my name, an invitation of twinkling wonders. There must be some place out there for me. It's like a happy dream.

Mister Pleats gives me a warm, wet lick.

I hug him close. For once, I feel like I could belong to something else. I could find it. Maybe I ain't such a crumb, after all.

AFTERWORD

So there I was in an anthology group. 50 some fiction writers meeting up in Las Vegas sometime in January, 2019. Before attending, the group was challenged to write short stories. No more than 6,000 words each. Most any genre was allowed unless specified. Eight story themes. And only one week to finish each one, revise them and submit every last word to the editors for consideration. On top of that, I'm battling with my introverted self, forcing myself to go to a place that attracts crowds.

Fortunately, no rowdy gang of gamblers tied me to a chair and forced me to play slots all night. Most of each day was spent in a conference room. Writers sat two or three to a table. Everyone hoping—like me—to sell at least one story. And as I've discovered, many writers are introverted to lesser or greater degrees.

What surprised me after the anthology event was my renewed interest in science fiction. Somewhere along the way of my life, I forgot about my love for the genre. As a child, sci-fi books, movies and television were almost always at the top of my list of preferred entertainment. I was an awkward and shy kid, never really fitting in with the other athletes that populated the playground. So the science fiction genre showed me that it was okay to be an alien. Even if meant being an alien on the planet Earth where red swing sets and blacktop dodgeball were ruled by the uniformed play-masters of a private school.

But nothing could compete with an eleven-year-olds passion for J.R.R. Tolkien's *The Lord of the Rings*. Maybe this caused me to deviate from sci-fi in my late teens. Yet for the Vegas anthology group, I didn't write a single fantasy story as an adult. Paranormal? Yes. A romance? Yes. And the rest were sci-fi. No orcs and wizards appeared anywhere. And magic and necromancy never crossed my mind.

Not that I've never considered writing fantasy. I've touched on magical realism in previous collections of stories. If you've read my books *Bedtime for Seneca* or *A Cat Will Play*, you may be reminded of television shows like the *Twilight Zone*. Some of the stories in those other books seem to straddle somewhere between fantasy and sci-fi. But I swear that I've never gone all the way into a world where fire-breathing dragons terrorize small villages.

I've pondered my January results with the anthology group. It seems that there is someone I've forgotten about. That shy, awkward kid is still hanging out on that private school playground from so many years ago. And it's evident from this collection, *The Sound of Blue*.

I'm not exactly sure how the "Last of Lasts" came to be. The theme for that anthology group's week was *explorers*. Most readers may think of exploration as a physical activity. But why not explore the mind? So that's where I went. My one brother suffers from schizophrenia, so perhaps I was trying to reach out to him through a story. He's not easy to reach even when standing face-to-face with him and trying to have a conversation. Do you know someone with schizophrenia? It can be heartbreaking.

"Waking from an Eternal Sleep" is a story about secrets. It's a secret stacked on top of another. To be honest, the story's theme is really a twist on the classic sci-fi theme of humans in a zoo. I don't feel like "Waking" offers too much twist of the theme. But please don't write me emails if you don't like the story.

Now, the two stories that really got me excited to write are "Jump Trains and Simultaneity" and "The Sound of Blue." Both spoke to my inner self and that child-like feeling of being alien. In the first story, Bobby the shoeshine boy is a kid that doesn't fit in. He's getting by but no one really takes notice of him. And he's aware that if he vanished from the Oberon Galaxy, he'd be forgotten in a nanosecond. I wonder if anyone noticed when I had graduated from eight grade.

"The Sound of Blue" involves another type of alien— the android. A mechanical humanoid is a technology that begins to take us into a place known as the uncanny valley. That's a place where an object imperfectly resembles a human being. And the effect can be eerie, even sometime revolting.

But I didn't want the reader to be revolted by Marky VI. What I wanted to do was make the android feel like the alien in the story. The only way that I could fully accomplish this was to give the android some connection to humanity. The transition from machine to human-like was the tricky part. After all, how can we feel alien if we can't at least have some feelings?

So now I'll finish up my rambling and pose a question or

two to you. Was the android Marky VI actually alienated? In the end, was he brought closer to the people he served in function? Only you, the reader, can decide that.

ABOUT THE AUTHOR

Michael is the author of several collections of short stories. Under pen name M. Duda, his titles include We Dream at Twilight and Whispers from the Grave.

He most recent story, "The Sound of Blue" won Silver Honorable Mention from Writers of the Future. This has fueled his passion for writing fiction.

He lives in Ohio with his wife, three dogs and two cats. He writes because his cat hates him. You can find out what he's up to at www.authormichaelduda.com.

ALSO BY MICHAEL DUDA

Whispers from the Grave

Deny the Father

We Dream at Twilight

Tiny Stories

Bedtime for Seneca

Printed in Great Britain
by Amazon